Lunch with Harry

"When I find out what I want,

I'll let you know"

by

Tony Drury

Novella
Nostalgia

Published by City Fiction

ISBN: 978-1-910040-10-2

LUNCH WITH HARRY

"Ja. Ik ben een idioot!"

Ella van Houten expressed her frustration in her native tongue. If she kept her patients waiting thirty minutes (which occasionally happened) she would expect them to be annoyed. So how was it that the oldest toy shop in the world did not open its Saturday doors to the general public until 9.30am? She should have checked before catching an early morning tube train from Harrow into London's Oxford Circus. She had used the eighteen-stop journey to read more about the Texas War of Independence.

She scanned the relatively quiet traffic lanes of Regent Street leading south to Piccadilly Circus. Again, she checked the information given on the imposing entrance. She had no choice but to occupy herself for the twenty-seven minutes wait she now faced. She had to be at the West End clinic by 10.30am. What should she do in the remaining twenty-six minutes before Hamleys opened its doors?

She had a thought and started giggling to herself. She heard the music of 'Moon River' introducing the opening scene. And there, in Manhattan, was Holly Golightly wearing shades, a full-length black dress and a heavy pearl necklace. She was looking into the window of Tiffany's, the jewellery store on New York's Fifth Avenue. Ella shrugged her shoulders. What did the legendary actress Audrey Hepburn have over her? Her body mass index was currently 24.6 so the first answer was about sixteen pounds in weight. Miss Hepburn was slim and sensational with her black hair swept back into a bun and adorned by a silver tiara. Ella's was fair, cut short and tidy but it was also practical, which was important.

Ella pouted her lips, recalling the facial expressions that made Audrey Hepburn's portrayal of Holly so mesmerising. She moved on down the street and peered into the window of a dress shop. She saw her reflection and tried to impersonate the film icon. But something important was missing. Looking around, she spotted a cafe. She went in and bought a coffee and a croissant. Returning to the shop she tried to reprise the early morning scene at the opening of 'Breakfast at Tiffany's.' What had Holly been thinking as she ate her pastry? Possibly she was lusting after men; the wealth and privilege that they represented.

She pondered the calorie count of her breakfast and promised herself that she would adhere to a strict regime starting on Monday. She looked back at her reflection in the window. She hoped that she shared Hepburn's looks. Numerous men had told her that she was beautiful. A disciplined, semi-vegetarian diet meant that her skin was in pristine condition. The occasional session exercising at the local gym, under the tutelage of one of the trainers, was achieving excellent muscle tone. She laughed to herself. Hepburn had been naturally thin. She dropped the paper bag and empty coffee cup into the trash bin. She began to stroll back to the store, which opened at 9.30am on a Saturday morning.

In the Netherlands it was nearing 10.30am. In a bedroom on the first floor of a modest house in Haarlem, North Holland, Ella's brother was dying of what was being diagnosed as a wasting disease. He was unmarried. He had his parents and younger brother to look after him in the family home. He was thirty-two years old.

Ella returned to Hamleys and wiped a tear away from her eye: she had switched from thinking about Holly Golightly and was now seeing Marius. Her English-born mother had pushed her to study for medical school and was a prime reason she ended up at Newcastle University, graduating in 2004. Ella had, in fact, first suggested that Marius should consult a doctor after she became concerned by his inability to button his shirts. She watched him struggle to swallow and when he stumbled outside their house she booked the appointment herself. During the week when she returned to her duties as a general practitioner in West London there was no news. She arrived back home to hear the results of his examination. He was in hospital undergoing further tests. It was thought that he was suffering from amyotrophic lateral sclerosis, a random killer from which few victims survive after five years.

It was because of Marius that Ella now had ten minutes to wait before the doors of Hamleys opened to the public. As a doctor she knew that there was nothing that could be done for him apart from unlimited family love and pain management. It was a minor relief that the disease did not affect the bladder and bowel muscles so his carers had only to help him to reach the toilet.

She tried to travel home every two weeks, which was why Ralph had left her. In the end, and with the agreement of the London clinic where she undertook locum work every other weekend, she managed to meet her obligations.

Her parents, Stijn and Elizabeth van Houten, failed to recognise the onset of Marius's depression. For them, it was heart-breaking watching their son wither away. It needed the medical practitioner to understand how alive he still was, and that his treatment mattered if her brother was to enjoy some quality in the life remaining for him. This led to Ella taking an interest in his collection of toy soldiers. From an early age Marius studied global warfare and had persuaded his father to board over the loft so he could set out some of the battles in American history. There were figures everywhere and Marius knew each and every one. It was a chance remark that led to the search for Santa Anna.

It followed their first and only row. Her brother had used the phrase "before I go" and Ella had shouted at him. They ended up in each other's arms agreeing never to refer to his pending death again. She could not resist asking him what he had been going to say. His eyes lit up.

"Ella. Do you remember when we watched 'The Alamo' together?" He hesitated as she wiped away the spittle from his lips.

"John Wayne led the defenders of the mission against President General Antonio de Santa Anna." He was becoming more animated.

"February 1836," he said. "The Texas Revolution."

Ella laughed.

"Marius," she cried, "you know your history books."

"Ella," he responded, "Santa Anna massacred all the defenders!"

Marius had collected forty-two of the forty-three piece set battle. He was missing Santa Anna. He had sought the advice of various societies but no one was able to help him.

Ella looked at her watch and noticed that other shoppers were arriving. There were five minutes to go before she could enter Hamleys and ask for their help in finding a Mexican General. She then trod on Harry's foot.

"Phew, thank goodness you're slim," said a pained voice.

The five orange-coloured canopies overhanging the front of the toyshop and covering various window displays were designed to entice a younger audience. There were eight adults and a number of excited children waiting for the doors to open. In addition, a woman with an arthritic back, who was retaining her balance by relying on walking sticks in each hand, seemed out of place.

Ella sought out the source of the exclamation. When she focused on his face she was immediately disarmed by the stranger who was flexing his foot. He was also hobbling to one side to allow other shoppers to push forward as they anticipated the opening of the doors.

"A few more pounds and I'd have been off to casualty," he laughed.

The second feature that Ella noted was his beige jacket and open-neck white shirt.

"Are you sure you're…?" she spluttered.

They were distracted by the doors of Hamleys being opened and the customers surging through as they attempted to keep up with their families.

The stranger was around six inches taller than Ella, who was five-eight. He was unshaven, although Ella could smell that he was wearing cologne. She estimated that he weighed around one hundred and eighty pounds.

"So, how are you going to apologise?" he laughed.

"Oh," said Ella. She looked at her watch. She had less than an hour to locate Santa Anna and reach the clinic in Mayfair where she would be advising wealthy hypochondriacs on their optimum route to longevity. They would, of course, ignore her strictures but all that mattered was that they paid their bills. Her parents had limited funds and she was sending money to them every two weeks for Marius's care.

"Do I need to do that?" she asked. She sensed what was happening as his eyes surveyed her from top to bottom.

"No. Not at all," he said.

She loved the flecks of grey in his hair. He had a small scar on his chin.

"I'll buy you a double Americano," she smiled. "It's the least I can do". She stepped back and stared at him.

"There's some Ralph in you," she said to herself.

He looked down at her and seemed to be annoyed.

"The least!" he exclaimed. "I'm suffering from a bruised toe: I may need surgery." He put his hand on her shoulder. She left it there. "The least I'm prepared to accept is that you accompany me to Fortnum and Mason so I can buy you a glass of champagne." He squeezed her shoulder. "Please," he added.

Ralph used to do that when he wanted Ella to sense his oncoming passion for her. Santa Anna could wait, but not her weekend patients; she needed to send some money to Holland on Monday.

"My best offer is a coffee," she said. "In truth, it's my only offer." She removed his hand. "And it gets worse. I will be calling for a taxi at ten minutes past ten."

As he pretended to radiate a childish face, she playfully slapped him.

"GBH and a broken foot," he cried.

They crossed over Regent Street and began the short walk to the coffee house.

"I'm Holly," stuttered Ella. "No. No I'm not," she corrected. "I'm Ella."

"Two for the price of one," he said.

"Who are you?" she asked.

"Harry."

"No, you're not," she said.

He seemed surprised but she was looking ahead.

"I was christened Henry but everyone calls me Harry," he chuckled as he opened the door and pointed to a vacant table.

Ella hesitated and remained standing.

"You're not Harry," she said.

"Oh. So who am I?"

"You're Fred."

He sat down and watched Ella order and wait for their refreshments. He was not asked what he wanted. She had her bag with her but had left a book on the table. He picked it up and looked at the cover: *'The Alamo' (1836): Santa Anna's Texas Campaign' by Stephen*

L. Hardin. He began to read the back page notes but quickly put it down. He was intrigued by her choice of reading material.

She returned to their table carrying a rather full tray: she watched his face as he spotted the *pain au chocolat* she had added to the order for their coffees. The early May warmth meant each of them had foregone coats. He thought she was perhaps over-dressed for a weekend morning. He lifted the pastry to his mouth. Ella had asked for it to be heated. As a consequence, a piece of warm chocolate dribbled down onto his shirt.

Ella started to laugh as she grabbed at a paper tissue and attempted to clean up the mess.

Harry watched and then gently pushed her away. He was warming to her.

"As a basis for our unexpected friendship," he said, "you have bruised my foot, slapped my face and attempted to poison me."

"Fred did not start too well," Ella chuckled as she sipped at her coffee.

"Fred," he said. "Let me hazard a guess. He was the man of your dreams who let you down." He placed the pastry on his plate and cut it into small pieces. He watched as she cleaned her hands with a wipe: there was no ring on any of her slender fingers.

"That was Ralph," said Ella, "he walked out on me twelve weeks ago."

She waited for the inevitable reaction – 'He must have been mad!' – or something similarly patronising, as the male predator attempted to establish his base for the inevitable emotional assault.

"Perhaps you were not what he wanted," commented Harry.

Ella stared at him.

"I had choices to make: it was difficult," she said.

Harry consumed the final piece of his breakfast without further mishap.

"Did Ralph make the right choice?" he asked.

She bowed her head and stirred her coffee.

"So, who is Fred?" he continued.

"You're Fred," laughed Ella. She finished her drink and reached for the glass of water on the tray. "I didn't realise that Hamleys doesn't open until 9.30am on a Saturday and I had thirty minutes to occupy myself." She blushed. "So I imagined that I was Holly Golightly arriving at the jewellery shop at the start of 'Breakfast at Tiffany's'."

Harry stared at her. "And Audrey Hepburn played Holly," he said.

"Yes. She was stunning," sighed Ella.

Harry paused and thought carefully. "If I was to say that you are most certainly as beautiful as Audrey Hepburn, I suppose you might start distrusting my motives," he suggested.

"Definitely", said Ella. "But please don't stop trying."

Harry was stirring his half-empty coffee cup. He could not take his eyes off her face.

"And Fred?" he asked.

"The actor George Peppard," said Ella. "He played opposite Hepburn. He was the love interest. He was a writer called Paul Varjak."

"So who was Fred?" asked the perplexed companion.

"Holly called him Fred. It was the name of her brother who was in the army. She was a bit crazy."

Harry smiled.

"Are you crazy?" he asked.

"We're all crazy, Harry," said Ella.

Harry wiped his forehead.

"So what's this thing you have about 'Breakfast at Tiffany's'?" he asked.

"When I want to cry I watch the movie," replied Ella. "The ending, as they kiss in the pouring rain: I weep buckets, every time." She drank some water. "Can you remember the music?" she asked. "You can't, can you." She smiled. "Moon River." She looked at her watch. "I must go." She frowned. "I'm not going to find him, am I?"

"Fred?" suggested Harry.

"Santa Anna," said Ella.

"He wasn't in 'Breakfast at Tiffany's'," laughed Harry.

"Can I have your mobile, please?" she asked.

He handed it to her. She pressed some digits and gave it back to him.

"Now you have my number." She stood up. "Goodbye, Fred," she said as she prepared to hail a taxi.

"But we've not talked about me," pleaded Harry.

"So we haven't," laughed Ella as she strode towards the door. She wondered what he really meant. Was he flirting with her? She thought not. She sensed an inner integrity about him. But, there again, perhaps he was being the male predator.

Several days went by and the memories of Harry were quickly overtaken by crowded surgeries and emails from home. However, on Thursday, early in the afternoon, she received a text message.

"Can u meet Sat. 1.00pm Covent Garden? Fred aka Harry."

She was due to cross under the English Channel and travel by Eurostar to Holland. She exchanged messages with her father and requested more information about Marius's condition. She then spoke to her senior partner at the surgery in Harrow and asked if she could have Monday off her clinical duties. He immediately agreed to her request. She sent her reply.

"Yes. Need to be at St. Pancras by 3.30pm."

She did not receive a reply until after ten o'clock that evening. She grabbed at her phone.

"I've watched the film. Holly was crazy. She played games with Fred. It's a deal."

Ella picked up her wine glass, drank deeply and sighed with anticipation.

The following morning, after she had tried to help an overweight teenager with stomach pains, she glanced at her phone.

"Table booked. Carluccio's, St. Pancras. 1.00pm. Fred."

She prepared her reply as a patient needing a hip replacement came in to ask why the hospital wait for his operation was now ten months.

"I'll check again, Mr. Abrahams," she said. "I'm sorry. I don't want to increase the pain killers because of the wear and tear on your stomach lining." What she did not say was that there was little point in her contacting the hospital as they would take no notice of a representation from a local GP. She looked askance. Her patient had left her room thanking her. She had done nothing for him. She returned to her texting.

"Holly will be looking her best."

After failing to help the tolerant, pain-wracked seventy-two year old, she called in her next patient.

She groaned as she realised that Mrs. Ringrose was on her way in. She just had time to hear her mobile buzz. She read his response.

"Minimum of fuss, maximum of flavour."

She dashed off her reply.

"Well, Fred, you sure know how to excite a girl."

Immediately, the reply came in.

"That's how Carluccio's describe themselves."

As she laughed to herself, Mrs. Ringrose sat down and wanted to know if Dr. van Houten intended to take her symptoms seriously. Ten minutes later, much to Ella's professional relief, she realised that her patient might be suffering from Graves' disease. Ella explained how the thyroid worked and the problems caused by excessive hormone production. She said she had noted her sleeplessness, irritability and some muscle weakness: she needed to take a blood test but she was fairly certain about her diagnosis. As the depressed patient expressed her thanks, Ella looked at her. What she did not tell her was that the main indication was her bulging eyes.

"Mrs. Ringrose," she smiled, "you and I will fight this together. We'll do our best to get you well again."

As the door closed, Ella picked up her mobile phone and scrolled to her diary and down to Saturday. She keyed in *'Lunch with Harry.'*

He was friendly from the start as he handed her a single red rose. He had chosen well. Carluccio's, situated on the Grand Terrace of St. Pancras International Station, was busy but he had reserved a table for them. The staff soon took care of Ella's luggage.

They were seated, and she smiled at him as she

smelt the flower. There was then a silence which was relieved by the waiter bringing them a plate of focaccia topped with grilled aubergine.

Ella groaned. She had not checked her weight for several days but the belt around her waist told its own story. She made an immediate decision. Her unbreakable diet would start on Tuesday morning when she was back from Holland. She did not understand, at this juncture, that Harry preferred women who carried a few extra pounds. She was not to know that he had become frustrated as he had watched Vicki run and run in her attempts to be slim. He and Ella had already spent enough time together for Harry to work out the curves.

They indulged in small talk while she scanned the menu and selected bruschetta with a tomato and feta topping followed by homemade ravioli. He shared her choice of the starter and requested a bistecca di manzo. A bottle of Pinot Grigio was brought and the waiter poured them each a glass.

Harry lifted his and said, "To Holly."

Ella gave him an Audrey Hepburn smile and touched his glass with hers. She liked his decision to come clean-shaven.

"To Fred," she proposed. "The last time we met you were complaining that we had not talked about you," she said.

Harry groaned. He had so many questions to ask. Who was Ella? Why was she outside Hamleys? What was this thing about Santa Anna? Why had Ralph walked out? Why were they meeting at St. Pancras? He decided to leave 'Breakfast at Tiffany's' alone.

"I think you make lots of money," said Ella.

"Does money matter to you?" he asked.

She thought about Marius and the cost of his care.

"Answer the question," she ordered.

"Things are good. I work in the City."

Ella decided that she'd let Harry dominate their early conversation. She made some progress by establishing why he was outside Hamleys. He explained that he was buying a birthday present for his son who was being brought up by his grandparents: he told her that his wife had died two years ago.

"She was so fit," he said, "she ran five miles every morning. It came right out of the blue. You won't have heard of it: ARVC." He ran his hand across his forehead. He was distracted by the arrival of their order.

"Arrhythmogenic Right Ventricular Cardio-myopathy," said Ella as she moved around her plate and utensils. She picked up the salt cellar, put it down again, and moved aside to allow the waiter to sprinkle grated pepper over her food.

Harry looked at her with a look of amazement.

"I'm a doctor, Harry," she said.

"But Holly was…"

"Holly was a crazy Manhattan socialite. There was a suggestion she was a hooker. She also wanted to be a film star. It took Fred to straighten her out." She sipped at her wine. "I'm a rather ordinary Dutch-born everyday GP."

"But your accent?" he said.

"English mother."

He looked at her with an intensity which Ella had not seen before in him.

"I never understood what ARVC really is. Vicki went so quickly," he said. "There was so much to do,

14

and George, understandably, took the loss of his mother very badly."

"Had you not seen the signs?" she asked. "To be fair, it is difficult enough to diagnose it in the surgery."

"What signs?" he asked.

"Put simply, the cells of your heart muscles are bonded together by proteins. Patients with ARVC suffer from under-developed proteins. In other words, the heart muscles cannot do their job of pumping the blood around the body." She paused to drink some water. "The body, in its practical way, builds up fatty tissues in an attempt to repair the damage. Not always, but usually it's the right side of the heart, the ventricle, that's affected. It becomes thin and stretched. The problem is, as I said, that the blood is not being pumped properly."

"Thanks, that helps," he said.

"The survival rate is quite high, which is no good to you." She put her hand across the table and held his arm. "I would need to look it up to get the exact figures but most people will have seen their doctor before it's too late. Did Vicki not get palpitations? What about breathlessness?"

"I put those things down to her daily run. We had George, and then she decided no more children. She became obsessed about her figure."

"Swollen ankles?" asked Ella.

"She took so many baths I rarely saw them," answered Harry.

Ella frowned. "There is a condition. We call it a 'hot phase.'"

"Hot phase?" he asked.

"We don't understand why, but ARVC victims can

sometimes suffer from unexpected cardiac arrest. Where was Vicki when she was taken ill?"

"She was out running. George was with his grandparents. I was working. I was called to the hospital. She died the next morning."

"I'm so sorry, Harry," she said as she finished her drink.

He immersed himself in a second bottle of wine that appeared after the waiter had cleared away their plates. They were indoors at Carluccio's, although he could see that most of the platform tables were occupied.

"There is something else about ARVC, Harry," Ella said.

"Need I know any more?"

"It might help." She paused and drank some wine. "It's an inherited condition. Perhaps you should get your son checked out."

He stared at her.

"I wish someone had told me that. Her bloody mother, no doubt."

"Don't rush to judgement, Harry," she said.

He almost choked. "Was she the source?" he wondered to himself.

It was at this point that their conversation began to wander. Ella was asking herself if she had been too prescriptive in her explanation of Vicki's medical condition. Harry was reliving the humiliation he felt from a failed marriage; Ella had yet to understand that. Their plates were cleared away and neither wanted any gelato that the waiter seemed keen to serve them.

"So, was Holly an expert on the Texan War of Independence?" he asked.

Ella laughed in relief. She was worrying that they were drifting. "That would have been Fred," she replied. "He was the author."

"With a cheque for fifty bucks," cried Harry. "That scene in the film when they went into Tiffany's to try to buy Holly a present for ten dollars!"

Ella leaned across and kissed his cheek.

"So, tell me Dr. Ella… er…" stuttered Harry.

"Dr. Ella van Houten," she said.

"I've read up on it," replied Harry. "Santa Anna was the Mexican General who wiped out the Alamo."

She leaned across the table so that they were closer together. She told him about her brother Marius and his terminal condition, but chose to omit the medical details. She confided in Harry that she would not rest until she had located Santa Anna and completed his battle scene.

"So, last Saturday…"

"Last Saturday I was going in to Hamleys to ask for their help in finding the missing piece," Ella smiled, "but this man diverted me."

Harry told her that he did have a bruised toe and offered to show it to her. She said that she thought that was not necessary as they laughed together. He then seemed puzzled.

"But why did we not go back to Hamleys after our coffee together?" he asked.

"And be seen with a man who had spilled chocolate down his shirt!" said Ella.

She continued by explaining that every two weeks she undertook private medical duties at a West End clinic and told him what she earned. Harry admitted that he was impressed by her pay. He was jolted by her reply that it was hardly sufficient to pay all the medical bills. She looked intensely at him.

"Please do not offer me any money," she said to herself, "just don't do it, Harry."

Her train was leaving at 16.04, so she collected her luggage and she and Harry went to a bar; he had a scotch and she sipped a Drambuie on ice. She savoured the taste of honey and the scent of the herbs. They were relaxing together and yet, inwardly, both were hesitant. There were many more questions to be asked and answered but Ella realised that he was lost in his own thoughts. They parted with a cautious hug. Harry put his hands on her shoulders.

"Will you allow me to do something for you, Ella?" he asked.

She groaned inside. "You're going to ruin our lunch, Harry. I just know it. Here it comes: the condescending male gesture," she thought.

"Wat is het?" she snapped, lapsing into her native tongue.

"Will you allow me to go with you back to Hamleys?" he asked. "Let's find Santa Anna together."

She caught the Eurostar Express and three hours later arrived at Brussels Midi. She changed to the high speed Thalys train, and reached Amsterdam at ten forty-two. Her father was waiting for her and soon they were travelling down the N200 to Haarlem. By eleven-fifteen, she had embraced her mother and was cuddling Marius. As she tidied his sheets, she noticed that his collection of 'The Alamo' had been laid out on a table. She wiped away the spittle from his lips and tested the strength of his muscles. She realised that he was looking at the gap at the front of the

Mexican army and she felt a pang of regret.

She slept in her old bedroom. Her mother always had it ready for her. Her parents would attend to Marius during the night. As she rubbed her eyes, her phone signalled an incoming message. She looked at the text.

"Hamleys next Sat. 9.30am? Fred x."

She was too tired to compose a reply.

"Cool x," she responded.

She closed her eyes wondering with whom he was spending Saturday night. Was she attractive?

She used the return journey to London on Monday evening to think about ARVC. It simply did not add up: how did he miss the symptoms? Between reaching her flat in Harrow and seeing her patients the next morning, she managed five hours sleep. She quickly resumed her professional commitment when the first appointment of the day resulted in a man of eighty-two being dispatched to hospital with heart palpitations.

Around lunchtime she sought out her senior partner, Keith Goodwin, to thank him, once again, for allowing her the freedom to travel to Holland. He invited her into his room. As she sipped her coffee (and refused a biscuit) he asked her a question.

"Your brother," he began, "he's suffering from amyotrophic lateral sclerosis. Have you any doubts over the diagnosis?"

"None whatsoever, Keith," replied Ella, without hesitation. "I've read up on it and discussed Marius's condition with the consultant. We know to our cost that the motor neurone diseases can fool us but he's well advanced; it's a matter of months, even weeks."

Her colleague looked at her, a little quizzically.

"How much value would you and your family put on extending his life?" he asked.

Ella looked askance.

"Every extra day would be golden," she said.

He handed her a piece of paper. It had, written on it, a name and a phone number.

"Friend of mine. Runs a private clinic in Chesham. He's been testing a new drug. It's not yet approved but he's managing to give certain patients an increased period of life expectancy. He's treated ALS. I spoke to him. Ring him." He paused. "But we need to talk about something else, Ella."

She looked at the information given to her and thought about the possibilities opening up for Marius. She then realised that there was more to discuss. Dr. Goodwin's forehead was creased in concentration.

"What's troubling you, Keith?" she asked.

"This private locum work you're doing. Two weeks in four. Must you do it?"

Ella laughed and decided to eat a biscuit. "My parents cannot afford the cost of looking after Marius," she said. "My mother has given up work and retired; she was a librarian and receives a modest pension. My father is now working part-time and earning very little." She wiped her eyes. "Without my money they'll not be able to afford the prescriptions, the nurse and the consultant's bills." She picked up her cup and put it down again. "When he goes, I'll stop."

"We both know that weeks can become months," said Dr. Goodwin. "I accept you'll not let it affect your surgery work but, Ella ..." he paused, "it's Tuesday lunchtime and you're already tired."

"I must support my family, Keith. I really have no option other than to keep earning."

"I'd like you to consider stopping now," said her senior partner. "You're an important member of my team. You are overbooked more than any of us."

Ella stared ahead. "Are you saying my work…?"

"Quite the opposite. How much are you earning from your locum work?"

Ella laughed as she tried to ease the tension. "I'm paid per patient but usually it's around fourteen hundred pounds a session."

"In one day?" he queried.

"That's seven or eight wealthy neurotics," she smiled. "I consult from 10.30am to six in the evening."

Dr. Goodwin stared at her. "We'll increase your pay by three thousand pounds a month if you'll call it a day."

"But… what about…" she stuttered.

"I've had a meeting with the others and told them what I was proposing. Only one of your colleagues objected and she's been satisfied."

"More money?" suggested Ella.

"Of course," he replied. He stood up. "I saw Mrs. Ringrose yesterday evening. You were spot on. It's Graves' disease. I've sorted out her treatment. Do you want to know what she said to me about you?"

"Ik liever niet," she answered. The last thing she wanted was a patient complaint.

"She told me that she had walked out of here feeling better. It was because you told her that you'd fight the illness together."

"Don't we all say that, Keith?"

"You meant it, Ella. And Mrs. Ringrose hung on to that."

21

Later that evening, she tidied her flat. She decided to destroy the photograph of her and Ralph at the Last Night of the Proms. She reached for her phone and googled 'Restaurants, WC2.'

An hour later she sent a text.

"Change of plan. Sat. Table booked. 1.00pm. Bill's Covent Garden Restaurant. Agreed?"

His reply amused her. *"Harry books the lunches. Ja graag."* He most certainly agreed.

The days flashed by and Ella was surprised at her heightened anticipation of her lunch with Harry. On the Saturday morning she woke up to clear blue skies and a gentle south-westerly wind.

They spotted each other across St. Martin's Churchyard. It was a gloriously warm Saturday lunchtime. She was wearing an all-white dress, no make-up, and a band around her hair. She thought his choice of jeans, a lightweight T-shirt and jacket was stylish.

They embraced and decided to take a table inside.

"Good choice," said Harry.

"Their website says they're 'a smart and sassy affair'," laughed Ella. She kissed his cheek. "Could be referring to us, of course."

"To you, Holly. I'm a serious guy."

They were seated and the drinks were ordered. She gazed at her lunch date. "Okay, Mr. City Man, what do you do?" she asked.

"I trade the yen."

"Of course you do," she said.

"I have two partners. We run a hedge fund. We trade currencies. To make money you need volatility. In your language, we need prices to move as dramatically as possible. The dollar, the pound, the euro; they move against each other all the time. But there's too much money chasing them. We have identified certain currencies and we trade just four."

"The yen being one of them," she commented.

"The Japanese economy has been in deflationary territory for twelve years. We've made serious profits by treading where others fear to go."

A bottle of Frascati was placed on their table and the waiter poured them each a glass.

"What's happened to your clinic?" asked Harry.

Ella explained her change of circumstances.

He thought about what she had told him.

"Three thousand pounds a month increase!" he said. "They must want to keep you, Dr. van Houten."

Ella gave him a special Audrey Hepburn smile.

"We're off to Hamleys this afternoon," she said.

By the time the second bottle of white wine had been opened and the seafood linguini consumed, they decided to have ice cream in a few minutes time. Ella's commitment to a vague vegetarian diet had evaporated. She made a mental note to book a session at the gym. She would ask if Rohan was available; she liked his tactile style of training.

The waiter had returned and gone away again. Both their glasses of wine were replenished.

"ARVC," said Ella. "I'm still puzzled that you did not notice the symptoms."

Harry drank deeply.

"Yes, I realised that you were not going to allow me to mislead you."

"You were trying to fool me, Fred?" she questioned.

In the time it took for the ice cream to arrive,

Harry started to tell the story of his marriage. Ella was transported into a world with which she was to resonate. Her professional training was about listening and extracting the vital clues to the patient's condition. One of her friends in Holland, Ruth, had qualified to be a vet's vet. She was the consultant to whom vets referred the animals and their owners where they could not diagnose the condition. She told Ella that she could gain vital information by listening to the owner's observations about their pet before she started to examine the animal.

Ella had never forgotten what Ruth had told her. She listened intently as Harry took her into his world of relationships. She was initially baffled by his explanation of the 'Anna Karenina principles'. Inevitably, she silently related his theory to her time with Ralph. She was later to calculate that they had only scored four out of five, and therein lay the reason for the collapse of their partnership. She realised that Harry was now referring to the Russian classic.

In her youth she had read Tolstoy's masterpiece and she'd seen the film. But when Harry started to talk about the 'Anna Karenina principles' she was initially puzzled. But she held herself together and listened. Ruth would have been impressed as she absorbed his intensity.

Harry repeated the first line of the book: *'Happy families are all alike; every unhappy family is unhappy in its own way.'*

He continued by saying that a theory had evolved, based on Tolstoy's writings, to the effect that in every relationship, there must be compatibility with five factors: *Sexual attraction, financial matters, parenting, religious views, and in-laws.*

Ella quickly updated the categories and her alarm bells rang out like the peals of St. Petersburg cathedral. She ticked the first three boxes. She and Ralph could not take their hands off each other. They were both high earners and money had never been an issue. They had decided to have three children, two girls and a boy. She remembered the night they had consumed an excessive amount of red wine as he demanded she fix the sex of their children. She decided that perhaps religious views might be more 'political opinions' in today's world. She and Ralph agreed about nothing. She was in Europe and he was out. He thought that the Liberal Democrats would make a comeback. She thought he was mad but they always went to bed together.

It was the last of the criteria that finished them off. Ralph visited Haarlem on only one occasion and it went wrong. In truth, seriously wrong. He seemed unable to cope with Marius's condition and ended up arguing with Stijn van Houten. His departure was frosty and Ella shuddered as he hardly acknowledged Marius.

They had travelled back to St. Pancras, and on to Harrow, in almost complete silence. The situation was exacerbated by a deterioration in Marius's condition and Ella's decision to return the following weekend (at the cost of £1,400 earnings). She arrived back late on the Sunday evening to find Ralph sulking. They did not sleep together. Looking back, she realised the damage was done and it was only a matter of time. A week later Ralph left a rather petulant letter and disappeared; he suggested that she keep the flat and paid the mortgage herself. She made no immediate attempt to contact him.

She shook her head as she realised that Harry was still in full throttle. That had been Ruth's key point. It requires a total commitment to the other person's words. He was reliving his relationship with Vicki. Their future collapsed after George's birth. She had been in labour for around eighteen hours and came out of hospital to announce that they were having no more children. Harry felt he might get used to that but she was becoming closer and closer to her mother. They had to take George round to her parent's house at every opportunity.

Vicki also showed no appetite for returning to a sexual relationship. She became obsessed with her weight and took up road running. The months drifted by and they settled into an unfulfilled routine. The inevitable happened and he met someone else: a work colleague. He felt justified in cheating but, as the London nights with the younger woman increased in number and intensity, so he failed to realise that Vicki was struggling. She was returning from her runs in an agitated condition but Harry's mind was elsewhere. On the day that she collapsed he was in a Mayfair hotel with his love interest. His office inadvertently blew his cover. The letter he was later to receive from his mother-in-law was a tsunami of vitriol.

"I think at the end we perhaps ticked two boxes of the Anna Karenina principles. We never stood a chance." Harry looked out of the window and across the busy square.

"You missed the symptoms," she said, a little quietly.

"I know that, Ella," he replied.

Ella also looked out into the sunlit world outside.

"So did I," she said.

"Ralph?"

"Scoring five out of five seems a bit demanding, Harry." She put her spoon into the strawberry treat.

"We could take them one at a time," he suggested.

"I think that's what Holly would probably do," she laughed. "Let's go and find Santa Anna," she added.

They reached Regent Street and entered Hamleys. It was exceptionally busy and they were relieved to find a sales assistant who seemed genuinely enthusiastic about their search for Santa Anna. He was unable to locate a set of 'The Alamo' but took Harry's phone number and said he would make further enquiries.

They left the store, walked down into Piccadilly and on into Green Park. Ella noticed that Harry was trying to conceal his interest in the scantily clad women lying out on the grass so allowing solar power to begin the summer tanning of their skin. There was no discussion between them. Harry led the way and, after some essential shopping, they booked into a hotel. In the evening they went to the theatre. They sat close together as they watched 'Mamma Mia!' Afterwards, as she danced along the street, Ella sang a song from the show for Harry's benefit,

"Gotta put me to the test, Take a chance on me."

They closed the bedroom door and continued to discover that their bonding was becoming rather intense. In the next two weeks Ella was to experience what would happen when they tested the second of the principles exposed by the married Russian socialite and her affair with the rather affluent Count Vronsky.

By juggling her hours, Ella managed to arrange to

visit the clinic in Chesham during the early evening of the following Thursday. She was helped by Harry's offer to collect her and drive the eighteen miles from Harrow. He was delayed by the need to extract one of his traders from an over-exposed position, by over seventy million sterling, to the South Korean won which had suddenly turned against the pound. The dense commuter traffic added to their late arrival at around seven-thirty.

The old Victorian house was located down a gravel drive. Ella asked Harry to leave her alone to meet with the medical staff. He wandered off round the back of the building and walked down a tree-lined avenue that led to a small lake. He became lost in his thoughts. He was angry that the risk assessment programme had delayed, by over three minutes, highlighting the trader's mistake. His firm had lost two million pounds more than necessary as he unloaded the currency with European foreign exchange desks. The member of staff had been suspended and would be required to attend special training sessions. Harry was fairly certain she would come through successfully and return to her desk. She knew that her quarter's bonus payment was dead in the water.

It was a minor blemish in an otherwise profitable trading period. The yen was moving perfectly as Abenomics (Prime Minister Shinzo Abe's various attempts to drag the Japanese economy out of recession) resulted in its falling value. Harry's fund was up by sixty-four per cent and he and his partners had paid themselves a six-figure bonus ahead of the half-year results.

He looked up and saw Ella standing there. She

28

asked that they went for a walk. She explained to Harry that it was an ideal place for Marius to end his days and they could expect perhaps an extra three months or longer. She would speak to the consultant in Holland and arrange for his medical records to be sent to the clinic. There seemed little doubt that this solution was the best option for her brother. She would go to Holland on Saturday and talk it through with her parents.

Harry thought quickly. He would take George out for a boat ride in the local park tomorrow, late afternoon.

"Can I come?" he asked.

Ella looked at him and remembered back to the consequences of Ralph's visit.

"It's not an easy situation, Harry" she said.

He stared at her.

"No," she said inwardly, "you're not Ralph, are you, Harry."

"That would be wonderful," she said, "my mother is going to smother you."

But Harry could not understand why Ella seemed a little subdued. The true situation came out on the Sunday on their Eurostar journey back to London.

They had reached Haarlem the day before. Harry and Marius, together with his brother Stephan, bonded together and ended up going out to a local sporting event. Marius became distressed and they came back early. Stijn walked with his daughter in the park and, somewhat to his surprise, Harry found himself being taken by Elizabeth in a motor boat along the Spaarne River. She pointed out the Molen de Adriaan. Harry was absorbed by the carpentry behind the medieval windmill. As they returned home, she took his arm but said little. Later, he and Stephan went out, leaving Ella to explain everything to her parents and ponder their dilemma.

The train had passed through Lille, and Ella was gazing out of the window.

"I talked to Marius about his collection of toy soldiers," said Harry. "He really does know his battles. He told me the story of the Alamo: we must find Santa Anna for him before…" He told himself to make a phone call on Monday.

Ella turned and faced him. She seemed oblivious of the two women sitting opposite them. "Before it's too late."

"Do I sense that the visit has not been as successful as…?"

Ella kissed Harry and held his hand.

"We can't do it, Harry," she said. "My parents have signed up to one of these retirement home financing schemes. I was not fully aware of the true cost of Marius's care. They had been to two other consultants to try to find a cure." She took out a tissue and wiped her mouth. "My mother has become unusually tired so they have been paying for a nurse, specialising in pain management, to come in." She stopped and turned round completely so that she could talk to him more comfortably. "Their house is secure and they will stay there for the rest of their lives. They will simply leave me and Stephan very little inheritance, which we don't care about."

"I'm lost, Ella," said Harry, "your salary increase…?"

"They can pay for Marius's care now they have raised the extra money, Harry." She sighed, "What we can't do is find the four thousand pounds a week for the clinic." Her shoulders slumped. "I've made a dreadful mistake. I dangled the carrot of giving Marius a bit longer and then, when we worked out the financial requirements, we can't do it."

Harry's financial brain was racing. "How much longer will the clinic give him?" he asked. They were interrupted as the catering trolley came round. Harry asked for a brandy and ginger for both of them.

Ella sipped her drink but declined the peanuts offered by the steward. "We did our calculations on five months; twenty-two weeks," she said.

Harry calculated that they needed around seventy thousand pounds, and asked Ella if that was the correct figure. She said that there would be some savings. They had worked out they could probably make it work with fifty thousand pounds.

"I can find some more from my salary," she suggested, "and I think I might be able to remortgage the flat." She hesitated because she did not want to mention that her difficulty was that Ralph needed to sign the release forms and she could not find him.

"So you need fifty thousand pounds," Harry said to himself.

"Sorry, Harry," she mumbled. "I did not hear what you said."

They were travelling through the Channel tunnel, and Harry was thinking about the second of the Anna Karenina principles. There was an obvious solution, except he was undecided on the possible consequences. What he did know was that he did not want to lose Ella and she was, to say the least, unpredictable.

As the Eurostar Express pulled into St. Pancras

International Station, he was still uncertain as to what he was going to do.

Ten days later, Marius van Houten was settling into his private room in the clinic in Chesham. He had been brought over by ambulance with his parents following in their car. Ella was there to greet them and, after Stijn and Elizabeth had left for their hotel, she stayed and helped Marius to set up the battle of 'the Alamo' on top of the cupboard by the side of the bed.

She noticed that Santa Anna was still missing and groaned inwardly.

The days passed slowly for Harry despite the extended working hours as currency fluctuations gave his team the opportunity to trade the Argentina peso. He also found time to contact a salesman at Hamleys. He often checked for another message from Ella, hoping for an escape route from the one he had received.

"Leave me alone, please. Ella x."

Eventually she asked him to collect her. She stipulated where and when but offered nothing more.

"I know you have questions you want answering," said Ella as she sat down in the passenger's seat, "but can I please ask that you drive the car. We'll talk later."

They reached the private clinic in Chesham at around nine in the morning on a Saturday ten days after Marius had been transferred from Holland. To Harry's surprise, she asked if he wanted to come in and see her brother. As they walked down the carpeted entrance and corridor, Harry reflected on recent events.

When Ella arrived at the surgery on the Monday morning following their return from Holland, she had found waiting for her an envelope marked 'Confidential'. When she opened it she discovered a cheque for £50,000 and a note from Harry:

"To hell with Anna Karenina's principles. This is what Fred would have done. Love, Harry x."

Apart from the devastating message from Ella he had heard no more. He confirmed with his bank that the cheque had been presented for payment. Then, during the previous Thursday evening, she texted him and asked that he drive her to the clinic on the Saturday morning. That had given him enough time to plan his 'Fred' surprise.

As they reached the door to Marius's room, Ella stopped and put her hand on Harry's arm.

"He's not settled in very well. We think we underestimated the trauma of the journey."

Even before they reached the bed, Harry was stunned by Marius's gaunt appearance.

Ella was by his side and lifted his oxygen mask; she kissed him gently. He was semi-conscious. She then disappeared out of the room and returned with a nurse. Changes were made to the organisation of his bed and to the flow of liquids into his arm. The nurse muttered an apology and left.

Ella sat down and held Marius's hand: there was so little strength in it.

Harry's eyes went to the top of the bedside cupboard. There were the forty-two pieces of 'The Alamo'. Occasionally Marius regained some lucidity and talked to his sister. He recognised Harry and smiled.

They stayed for two hours and then left. As they returned to the car, Ella told Harry that she had seen the consultant on three recent occasions and he said it was a reaction to the change in circumstances and Marius should begin to recover within the next few days. They had not started the drugs regime because he was not yet stable. On one of the visits earlier in the week, Ella's boss, Dr Keith Goodwin, had accompanied her and later spoke to his friend, the owner of the clinic.

Ella looked across at Harry as she opened the car door. "I think he's struggling," she said.

As they travelled along the road to Harrow, Harry asked if she would accept his offer.

"Accept what offer?" said Ella.

"Fred's offer!" exclaimed Harry. "Champagne at Fortnum and Mason."

"I always wondered what you were doing outside Hamleys," she said. "You were on the lookout for innocent women who you could coerce into drinking champagne with you!"

"I was waiting to buy my son a present." He laughed. "But meeting Holly rather diverted me."

She leaned across and kissed his cheek.

They reached the main A40 into Central London and within twenty minutes they had parked the car in the Piccadilly area and were sitting inside Fortnum and Mason sipping a French premier wine.

"What did you mean," Ella asked, "stuff Anna Karenina's principles?" She hesitated but then did not wait for his answer. "I cannot think of how to thank you for the cheque." She lowered her eyes. "I wanted to tear it up but I had to think of Marius. I can't find Ralph so I'm unable to use my flat to raise some money."

"Which is why I decided to risk offending you," said Harry. "I realised it might affect us or, as Anna Karenina says, our financial compatibility."

"You mean our relationship," said Ella.

"You took the money but rejected me," he said.

"I made the decision to bring Marius to England. Because of you we can prolong his life." She lifted her eyes. "I just could not cope with anything else."

They had finished the champagne and Ella was sipping a glass of water.

"You must understand that I realised that," he said.

"Thank you," said Ella.

"I've a daft idea," said Harry.

"Cool. Here's to a silly idea," sang Holly.

He took out a twenty-pound note and waved it in the air. "That's as near ten dollars as matters," he said. "It's time for Fred to buy Holly a present."

"But Fred, I shop at Tiffany's. The airfare to Manhattan will cost thousands," she cried.

Harry took the menu and tore out a page. He told Ella that he was writing down a number of London locations. He held them in his clenched hands and told her to choose one. She picked it out and read the writing. "It says 'Old Bond Street'," she said.

They paid their bill, left the restaurant, and hailed a taxi. Before long they were alighting outside Tiffany's in Old Bond Street. They went inside and looked around.

Ella was dazzled by the displays of jewellery. She started to waltz from one display cabinet to the next. A man came up and Harry said he wanted to buy his friend a present. When he said that his budget was twenty pounds, the assistant replied that he loved a challenge. After making several suggestions he produced a decorated lapel pin.

Ella disappeared to view a display cabinet where the jewellery started at several hundred pounds. Harry nodded at the shop assistant. The man disappeared and returned with a package just as Ella re-joined them. He gave him a small package.

"That's exactly twenty pounds, sir."

Harry handed a gift to Holly. She opened it with a certain schoolgirl enthusiasm as she realised it was a pendant. She uttered a sound which had the characteristics of "phew …oh …wow …" and then read the etched wording on its plate: *Please return to Tiffany & Co, New York, 925.'*

"For me?" Ella exclaimed.

Harry winked at the assistant who, on Friday, had accepted a generous payment to secure his participation in the surprise for Ella.

She had undone two buttons of her white shirt and was arranging the pendant around her neck.

As they left the store, she put her arms around him.

"Fred, I'm going to wear it forever."

They kissed. As they walked down the street towards Piccadilly Circus, Harry threw some pieces of paper into a waste bin. They all had 'Old Bond Street' written on them.

"But Fred, that's not to say I won't take other things off," she teased.

Several hours later that is exactly what she did.

From the start, it was wild. Deep in Carnaby Street, in the West End of London, on a mid-week evening following their visit to Tiffany's, Harry's firm held its annual Christmas Party. Ella was baffled by the bizarre invitation but accepted without hesitation. Harry explained that he and his partners wanted their party to make an impact. A tradition had arisen, based on an idea from a junior trader, that by calling it a 'Christmas Party', but holding it in July, it not only set the tone for the evening but also would be memorable.

The Cirque le Soir was a perfect location. It was mayhem from the start, not least because of the lavish pre-event entertainment that Harry's staff had organised at a local hotel. As the group of around thirty traders and clients entered the dark, forbidding premises, and a near naked girl with a snake around her neck had thrown herself at Harry, Ella decided that this could be fun. There was music blasting out and she was sure she detected the sound of Prince. She smelt the drugs but decided that she was off duty.

A man in a leotard made a versatile suggestion to her. He quickly lost interest due to her lack of response. She decided to watch a cage inside which two handlers were playing with an obviously drugged tiger. A drag queen appeared at their table and seemed unsure whether it was a man or woman taking her attention. Or was it his attention? An enthusiastic fire-eater nearly set the premises alight.

Ella noticed that Harry was fully committed to his role as the host. He was circulating amongst his guests and was clearly a well-liked person. She tensed as several girls made it crudely obvious that they were open to offers. A magician appeared at the table, took Ella's watch, smashed it to pieces and gave it back to her in perfect working condition. Two dwarfs arrived and went through their mock fight while soaking up the sympathy of the watching revellers.

Harry appeared and grabbed Ella's hand before leading her to another section of the arena. They entered together into the 'Court of Zoltar' who promised to tell them their futures. The small cabin was soaked in incense. Zoltar moaned and groaned and studied Ella's life lines on her open palms. He spent less time looking at Harry's hands. He chanted a meaningless incantation and tried to look down Ella's blouse. They left ten minutes later, Harry one hundred and nineteen pounds the poorer, and Ella giggling uncontrollably. Zoltar predicted that they were going to find health and wealth and make many children together. He had sold Harry his book of astrological predictions. Ella wondered how long it would be before Harry found out that her birth sign was Gemini. Her June birthday had come too early in their association. She was happy for him to know her strengths included 'affection' and 'adaptability' but less keen that a weakness was 'inconsistency'.

She grabbed Harry and pulled him into a corner. Shouting to make her voice heard above the atomic sound of the live group now belting out a song called 'Shark Infested Baths', she asked Harry if he really wanted children. He shouted out 'three' and held up the same number of fingers; she hugged him in agreement. She paused – Ralph had wanted three children: two girls and a boy.

Harry was distracted by one of his partners insisting he met a client in another part of the premises. He was to be away for some time. Ella returned to her table, realising that the third of the Anna Karenina principles was now satisfied. She was listening to Adele singing 'Hello' and apologising for breaking his heart; she was blaming herself for their break-up.

She thought back to Ralph. She missed his embraces, his friendship. She had moved to West London to be with him. In their case four out of five of the Anna Karenina principles were secure. But he became jealous of Marius. He resented her shared affection. Was it her fault? She should have managed the tensions with greater empathy. But her beloved brother Marius, the person with whom she had shared her youth, was dying. Ella could never understand why Ralph had argued with her father. She had always thought he was a weak man although that did not stop her adoring him. She shrugged her shoulders; Ralph had gone and Fred was already replacing him in the most unusual circumstances.

He was standing there; he was probably from Eastern Europe. He asked her to dance. The music had now acquired an African beat and was very loud. She looked around and could not see Harry. She accepted his invitation. Within moments they were together on the small disco platform surrounded by coiling bodies. His hands were acceptably everywhere. She clung to his waist and allowed him to smother her shoulders with his lips. His hands went lower and squeezed. She was in another world and being transported into ecstasy. His eau de cologne was pleasant and familiar but enough. His hands moved again but he knew the territory. She felt excited and wanted more. He bent her backwards and his lips hovered over her chest where he discovered her pendant. He read the inscription and placed it back on her skin. The music changed and Paul Simon was singing about a bridge over troubled water. She tucked her hands down the back of his trousers. They became as close together as physically possible. She looked up to the first platform and saw that Harry was staring down at them.

At around one in the morning Harry found her and made it clear that they were leaving the club. They were driven back to Harrow in silence; the courtesy car driver closed the divide but that made no difference. Harry made a half-hearted attempt to persuade her to go back to his flat but she said she was on early morning duty. He stood at the car door and she pecked at his cheek. He was driven off and she went to bed.

Two days passed and then they made contact. The following Sunday they went walking in the Chiltern Hills. This followed a period of around three hours with Marius. Harry stayed for thirty minutes and then went into the grounds and sat down by the lake where he started to read the latest Lee Child novel. He put it down and thought about his son. Their time together, the day before, had proved to be a difficult Saturday. George wanted to talk about his mother and eventually they visited her gravestone. They went on to the RAF Museum at Hendon but eventually Harry asked George if he wanted to go home. As he stopped the car, outside his mother-in-law's house, his son leapt out and ran to the front door without looking back.

Ella was perplexed. They had still not started Marius's drugs programme. He seemed to lapse between periods of rationality followed by a fitful sleep. When she tried to interest him in 'The Alamo', he just closed his eyes. She observed he was having difficulty in swallowing. She spoke to the duty nurse and, an hour later, managed to review his notes with a resident doctor.

After leaving the clinic, they agreed that some fresh air would do them good, and they were now in an area known as Bryant's Bottom. As they strolled along the farm tracks, they started to discuss the political consequences of the European Referendum. The Conservatives were close to electing Teresa May as their new leader, and thus Prime Minister, and Labour continued their unique ability to self-destruct. It was, however, Harry's opinion that the economic outlook was declining. Interest rates had been cut, but output was falling and unemployment was creeping upwards.

Ella managed to firstly annoy, then irritate, and finally anger Harry with her accusations that it was his fault for voting 'out'. 'Brexit' was the cause of it all. If he had followed her patriotic stance and remained 'in', all would have been so much better. She walked straight into his trap as he reminded her that one, she did not have a vote, two, she was European and thus biased, and three…

"So what is number three, Harry?" she snapped.

As they turned a corner at the edge of the woods, they came across a group of walkers who were standing around a person lying on the ground. Several of the watchers were reaching for their mobile phones.

"She's drunk," cried a woman.

As she reached the individual, Ella asked them to

stand aside. She leaned over and then turned the person on their side. She checked her pulse, returned her to a resting position and started talking to the individual. She looked up at one of the phone users.

"Call emergency services," she said. "Tell them it's almost certainly hypoglycaemia and to call Air Ambulance. We need to get her to hospital."

"Hypo...what?" exclaimed the man.

"Diabetes, mate," said another. "Make the sodding call."

"I need some sugar," said Ella.

Several rucksacks were searched and a sachet of sugar was handed to her together with offers of bottles of water. Harry noticed that Ella was talking to the woman all the time.

"Seventeen minutes," called the man on the phone.

"Too slow," said Ella, "tell them that's not good enough."

The sound of a motorbike announced the arrival of a paramedic. He joined Ella and then immediately made a call. "Nine minutes," he said.

The helicopter arrived and the blades created a storm of dry summer grasses. Harry had taken off his jacket and was trying to shield Ella from the debris. Within minutes, the woman was stretchered into the air ambulance and was on her way to hospital. Ella brushed off the various words of approval from several of the bystanders.

She and Harry continued their walk until Ella asked if they could turn back.

"What were you talking to her about?" asked Harry.

Ella chuckled. "It was a mild attack," she said.

"She was a sixty-year-old widow and she had forgotten to take her medicine. She'll be fine," she smiled. "I was not taking any chances." She grinned and gave him a special smile, "It was Fred to the rescue!"

"All I did was to hold up my jacket," he said.

"She spotted the pendant and I told her our story …," Ella paused, "she thought you were rather a dish."

Dr. Keith Goodwin sipped his scotch and looked at his friend.

"So you're not going to start the treatment at all?" he asked.

"He's too weak, Keith."

"Have you told Ella?"

"No. She's coming in tomorrow to discuss Marius with me." He drank his vodka and tonic. "She knows, anyway."

"I wonder how she'll take the news."

Ella loved the sensation of his flesh next to her. She rolled over and lay on top of him.

"So, Harry," she said, "how is Anna Karenina progressing?" She put her fingers across his lips. "Before you answer, you should know that I am reading the novel, and Count Vronsky is not a patch on you." She kissed him again. "Let's tick the boxes; 'Sexual attraction' …"

Harry lifted himself onto his elbows. "No problem there. You find me irresistible."

Ella playfully slapped his face. "Two: 'Financial matters'," she said. She looked at Harry.

"I don't think there is a box big enough that would

allow me to thank you for what you did, Harry." She pretended to think intensely. "Number three: 'parenting'," she said. "We've agreed three children, so that's another tick."

"We could start now," suggested Harry.

"'Religious views'," said Ella. "We decided that in our world that means political opinions, and you have been unable to justify your ludicrous decision to vote 'out'." She pinched his arm and he moaned. "We'll tick that box as well," said Ella. "Which leaves 'in-laws'."

"There's something else we need to talk about," said Harry.

She knew that it was going to surface at some stage. She also realised that her best option was to tell the truth. She had wondered if she might deflect the issue by expressing her frustration that she had not yet managed to find Santa Anna.

"I never again want to see you that close to another man," said Harry.

What Ella was not going to tell Harry was that the man she had met at the Cirque le Soir had managed to find her phone number and had contacted her. They met and she had experienced a traumatic evening as she fought off his expectations. She had berated herself during the long taxi journey back to Harrow.

In many ways, the situation had been caused by Holly Golightly. Not only did Ella watch 'Breakfast at Tiffany's' for its emotional release but because she was secretly obsessed with Audrey Hepburn's figure.

Ella carried several excess pounds. Her body mass index had risen to 25.3. Harry loved the contours and she was young enough to maintain a seductive physique. In her daily work she dealt with a range of females, from young teenagers to sixty-plus-year-old wives looking for seduction and sex; they sought her advice and help about diets which would maintain their attractiveness. The issue was becoming significant for the medical world. She had read in a magazine that some women were put off from buying clothes in high street shops because of the trauma of seeing themselves in the changing room mirrors.

She had tried a range of food regimes (she thought this a better word than 'diet') but found salads and boiled fish failed to satisfy her cravings after a day in the surgery. Her vegetarian discipline rarely survived a week. She was using a home delivery service, as she feared being seen in a supermarket and spotted by her patients who might see her loading her trolley with processed foods. In line with a large percentage of the population, if she opened a packet of biscuits and tried to restrict her intake to one, or perhaps two…

Audrey Hepburn was extraordinarily beautiful with, for some, the perfect figure. The scenes in the film where the director had maximised the seductive power of Hepburn wearing a shirt and little else, were mesmeric. Ella watched with tearful envy.

Which was why, when she opened the envelope in her surgery and started to read about a new approach to 'healthy eating', she did not follow her usual procedure of propelling it towards the waste paper bin. She began to read and had to be reminded by reception that her next patient was waiting to see her. She put the article in her bag and, later that evening, poured a large glass of wine, prepared some cheese and biscuits, and began to read.

The central theme of the research summary was that conventional dietary advice was being challenged. Most of the information and advice that Ella gave out in her surgery was based on a low fat and high carbohydrate intake. She knew this but still read on.

'Biologically, a carbohydrate is a molecule consisting of carbon, hydrogen and oxygen. It is a synonym of the word 'saccharide' which includes sugar, starch and cellulose. Foods high in carbohydrates include cereals, bread, rice, potatoes, pasta and sugars. This means jams, deserts and pastries.'

"Well, thank you for that," she laughed but still she continued.

A concept gaining credibility with cardiologists is based on the idea of LCHF: low carb, healthy fat. By restricting the intake of carbohydrates the body has to use other fuels which it takes from the body's stored fats.

"Rubbish," Ella snorted, and poured herself a second glass of wine. The mantra of cutting back on fats, filling up on carbohydrates, and prescribing statins was sacrosanct in her world. She continued to read the medical research.

She began to be interested in the arguments in front of her. 'The enemy of good health is sugar. It is a component in eighty per cent of all processed foods. The situation is exacerbated by the fact that simple carbohydrates such as white flour, potatoes and rice are metabolised into sugar by the body. Without realising it, the average consumption of sugar per person, per day, is twenty-three teaspoons.'

She put the papers down and decided to drink a brandy. She carried on reading.

'A high sugar diet can trigger an overload of insulin which will impact on the metabolic health of the body.' She sighed. The research also revealed that sugar can result in cholesterol becoming more inflammatory thereby damaging the arteries.

Ella was now seriously interested. The other finding, which she gasped at as she related it to herself, is that the daily consumption of processed foods results in sugar spikes and the mood swings which individuals find so frustrating.

"I know that," she said. Yet she still continued absorbing the material.

'The second key belief is that the right fat is good for the individual. Patients had previously been instructed to drink skimmed milk, to cut the fat off bacon and to avoid eating butter, using instead a cholesterol-busting margarine. This ignores the reality that the body, to function effectively, needs natural fats. A United States university had reported that their research showed a tablespoon of butter per day, in the context of a low carb intake, promotes good health.'

Ella loved eating butter. A late evening piece of toast was nectar to her.

She finished off the glass of brandy, ate the remaining cheese and crawled into bed. She spent a few hours in a restless sleep. At four o'clock in the morning, she arose, dressed and re-read the article. She decided to immediately change her regime. Out went the carbs and in came cauliflower rice and courgette spaghetti with a Mediterranean use of natural oils. Eggs were back on the menu and breakfast (when there was time) became a three-egg omelette packed with vegetables. Olives, nuts, avocados and meat were all allowed.

One week later she was frustrated by the lack of progress. She had shed one pound, the mood swings were still around and she was eating too many biscuits. Before dressing for Harry's party she had stood on the scales, groaned and needed an extra notch in the belt of her dress. Her self-esteem collapsed.

When the man approached her and took her on the dance floor, something inside ignited her Holly Golightly tendencies. She so regretted it. It was crazy to even see him again. How could she explain LCHF to Harry?

Harry could not get the vision out of his mind. He was wracked with guilt and pain. He relived Vicki's final few weeks and could not forgive his irresponsible lusting for the young trader who had since left the firm. Again and again he saw George running away towards the front door. He conceived a plan and went over and over the details in his mind. To his surprise, Ella, after asking a number of questions, agreed. He wrote a letter to his mother-in-law explaining that he had met another woman and he wanted to introduce her to George. He read her reply and hardly believed her thoughts. She acknowledged that George was not happy. He was enjoying his nursery school and he had some good friends. She said that she was concerned that he spent long, solitary hours in his bedroom and went for spells without speaking to either of his grandparents. Harry shared all this information with Ella.

"Pizza Hut," she said.

"Why there?" he asked.

"He's four years old. He needs to feel familiar and

secure," she replied.

Marius was no better. They spent the morning with him. The battlefield of 'the Alamo' had been pushed away. He seemed to realise that his parents had arrived from Holland, and after a while drifted off into a semi-sleep.

They all left the room and sat down in the lounge area. Ella tried to answer their questions. Stijn and Elizabeth struggled with the revelation that the consultant was still withholding the drugs regime.

Harry stood up and said he was going to sit with Marius. As he entered the room, Marius was awake and trying to reach 'The Alamo'. Harry pulled the cupboard over to him and Marius smiled. His visitor reached for the bottle of water and guided the tube into his mouth. He then used a paper tissue to mop up the dribbling down his chin. Marius was pointing at the battlefield. Harry realised that he was trying to show him that Santa Anna was still missing.

He was sitting at the side of the bed holding Marius's hand when the van Houtens arrived back. Ella said that her parents were now taking over. She went over to Marius and hugged him. Mr. van Houten seemed in some distress; his wife was calmer. As they left the room, Ella turned back and waved.

They walked to the car making small talk. They decided to join the Sunday afternoon walkers on the north side of the Thames at Hampton. There was an almost complete silence in the car as Harry drove round the South Circular Road. They parked and were soon walking along the tow path. Ella decided that she had no choice but to confront the situation.

"Harry. My behaviour. I made a mistake," she said.

"It was a good party," he replied.

She stopped and waited for him to face her. Laughter came from a boat on the water. Passers-by were generally failing to control their children and their dogs.

"You're looking good, Ella," he continued as he tried to broach a reconciliation.

They continued their walk and she told him about the LCHF diet and her obsession with Audrey Hepburn's figure. They reached an ice-cream van; Ella mouthed "bugger" under her breath.

"Too thin for me," said Harry.

"What!" cried Ella.

"She got away with it because she was beautiful but men generally like some flesh on a girl."

"How much flesh?" she asked.

She waited while he purchased two large '99s' from the vendor. As her teeth sank into the chocolate, she felt a sense of relaxation course through her body.

"Stay as you are, Ella." Harry licked his ice cream. "I've realised that I'll just have to fight off other men. You're a beauty, Ella van Houten." He looked at her with the glint she so loved. "Tomorrow, a female patient comes in and asks for advice on losing weight. What will you do?"

Ella laughed. "I'll give her a dietary guidance sheet authorised by my professional body," she said.

Harry frowned. "Is that your best advice?" he asked.

"No idea. But it does mean I can't be sued."

They walked on and he asked if she was still reading Tolstoy's masterpiece, which was by the side of her bed.

"We've ticked four of the five boxes," he said, "but the theory goes that a successful relationship needs all five ticked." He paused. "In-laws," he said, "which I take to mean family. It went horribly wrong with Vicki."

Ella stopped and faced him. "Are we going wrong, Harry?" she asked.

"I'm not, but you are," he replied.

"What…what does that mean?"

He put his arms around her shoulders. "Marius is absorbing all your emotional energy. I'm fine with that. But…but when we are with him, I sense you are fighting other battles. You are worrying about me, as well."

Ella wiped her eyes. "Should I have brought him to London, Harry?"

"Yes. You've given him the chance of extra time. That must be right."

"He's failing, Harry."

"Strange things can happen, Ella. The medical staff seem to know what they are doing."

"I'm going to lose him, and I'm worried I'll lose you as well."

"Why?"

"I think it's the Holly in me," she said.

"Harry. Can you please stop the car?"

They were five minutes away from his mother-in-law's house. He pulled into a lay-by and turned off the engine. He faced his partner.

"Harry. This is Dr. Ella speaking" she said with a half-smile on her face.

"Sorry, doctor," laughed Harry, "I promise I'll cut down on my drinking."

She playfully slapped his face.

"George is just four years old," she said.

"He's mature for his age," defended Harry.

"He's never met me and will struggle to understand who I am."

"No, I've told him all about you."

Ella groaned.

"That's what I feared," she said. "Harry, please, we must give him space. Let him make his own assessments." She smiled and he weakened. "Do something that you're not too good at doing," she paused, and put her fingers over his lips. "Don't talk too much to him."

They collected his son and strapped him into the safety seat in the rear of the Mercedes. Ella lowered her visor and watched George look around him. They reached the Euston area and parked the car. Harry hailed a taxi and soon they were in Pizza Hut in the middle of Covent Garden. George selected his choice of pizza and watched as Ella asked him if he would like to go with her to select their drinks. He returned with a giant cup of Pepsi. Ella then chatted to Harry who was reaching a state of apoplexy with the ongoing state of filial silence.

Ella stood up and whispered into George's ear. He nodded his head in agreement. They went off to the salad bar together. Harry noticed that George was holding her hand. They returned with three servings of tomatoes, potato salad, savoury rice and lettuce. A few minutes later their pizzas were served and Harry suggested they cut up their dishes and shared them around.

George laughed.

"I don't like yours, Dad," he said.

They continued to eat their meal in the confines of the noisy restaurant. Ella asked George who was his best friend. He spoke with some enthusiasm about Megan. She looked at Harry and smiled. "Like father, like…" she thought to herself.

George watched as his plate was cleared away and announced he'd like an ice-cream volcano. Harry began to ask whether he had eaten enough and groaned as his shin was kicked.

The meal was finished and Harry took his son to the toilet. They returned and Ella indicated they should sit down.

"George," she said, "may I please ask you a question?"

He nodded his head.

"How would you feel if I gave you a present?" she asked.

"What is it?"

She reached into her bag and brought out a small parcel wrapped in brightly coloured paper. She handed it to him. George ripped it open and took a mobile-phone-shaped device out of the packaging. He was immediately engrossed in pressing the buttons. Harry picked up the cover and read the description. It was a 'DigiGo': its main function was to allow kids to stay in touch with their parents. It offered the 'Kid Connect' app. It was coloured blue.

George looked at Harry's partner.

"What's your number, Ella?" he asked.

She snuggled up to him and kissed his shoulder.

Harry threw back the sheet and put his hand underneath Ella's chin.

"The third Anna Karenina principle," he said, "I'm

thinking it can be adapted."

"Tell me more," said Ella.

"We need only have two children," he said.

"But you want three," she said, although she knew what he was contemplating.

"We already have one," said Harry. "How would you feel about being George's mother?"

"I can never be that," she said.

"You know what I mean," he said.

She put her hands on his cheeks.

"Yes. I've been thinking along similar lines but…"

"It's asking a lot," said Harry.

Ella sat up and told him that they must think carefully. George had already been through so much disruption in his early life and, if they were not careful, they could disturb him again. She said that they would be morally wrong to create a level of expectation in George and then let him down.

"You have doubts?" asked Harry.

"We've both made mistakes" she answered. "We must feel able to tick all five boxes."

Briefly, she felt the pressure of the conflicting demands of Harry, Marius and now George. She prayed for an answer to her conundrum.

The consultant almost bowed his head as the family of Marius van Houten made their decision. Stephan, the younger brother, had arrived that morning and needed to return to Holland in the evening. His mother and father were now coming to terms with the inevitable. Marius had a lung infection, as his muscles were no longer functioning effectively. Ella made a brief examination and placed her ear on his chest. There was, in truth, only one option: the process of pain management was intensified.

The consultant anticipated their final request by nodding at Ella. "Dr. van Houten understands the answer to your question." He paused and hesitated, "We don't know the answer. In my estimation perhaps a week but amazing things can happen." He paused. "My advice is that you should try to remain nearby because I can only imagine how tiring it must be for you travelling back and forth to Holland."

Marius's mother gave way, and her husband led her out of the room. Ella stood by Stephan.

"We're glad we tried," he said. "Thank you for having Marius here with you."

In the days that followed, Harry read the situation correctly. He sent occasional texts but made no personal comments. He was disappointed that she did not reply but felt defensive after her statement about their mistakes. His colleagues noticed that he seemed to be trying to contact a man in the United States which was unusual: the firm did not trade the dollar. They heard him use the word 'FedEx'. They were not aware of a call he had received, the previous week, from a salesman working at Hamleys.

Ella attended to her clinical duties with her usual resilience. She always tried to keep in mind that, however trivial the symptoms, to that patient the pain and worry were real. Her senior partner wanted her to take time off but she preferred to maintain as normal a routine as possible. She went to the clinic every evening. There was no more to be said as they watched Marius lose his battle.

She thought about Harry, and finally texted him.

"Fred. I adore the pendant. Love, Holly x."

It was a wet and warm late July afternoon when Ella received a call from the clinic. Torrential rain was crossing the southern counties of England. Her father told her that Marius's condition had deteriorated further and she should get to them as soon as she could. There were two more patients to see and an unanswered text on her mobile. Within half an hour, and as she closed down her computer, she sent a brief message telling Harry that she was on her way to the clinic. The final words of her text were brutal:

"I need space please, Harry."

She was then asked to see a woman who had rushed into the surgery holding a damaged hand. Ella dressed the wound and waited until the ambulance arrived. She was delayed by forty minutes.

As she parked in the clinic car park and headed for the entrance, a wet, bedraggled figure approached her.

"Not now, Fred," she pleaded.

He looked at her but said nothing. As she moved away, he took out a small package and thrust it towards her. She put it in her pocket.

"Later, Harry," she said.

When she opened the door to Marius's room she knew that his end was near. Her parents were gazing out of the window. Stephan had delayed his return journey and was sitting with his brother. She quickly organised them by suggesting that they went to the guest rooms and tried to rest. She kissed her mother, hugged her father, and put her arms around her brother. She was then alone with Marius.

He was awake. She checked his tubes and adjusted the oxygen mask. She began to talk to him about their time together in Haarlem as siblings, and slowly a smile appeared on his face before his eyes closed and he drifted away again. The wall clock told her it was four-thirty. At a few minutes past five, the consultant walked in. He examined his patient and then indicated that he wanted to talk to Ella. They stepped outside, and she accepted his conclusion that it was now a matter of hours. She said she would leave her parents to rest. Two hours later, Marius's breathing changed, and Ella called in her family.

She held his hand as he fell in and out of semi-consciousness. But he clung on to life and, after the doctor had examined him, it was agreed that Stijn, Elizabeth and Stephan would return to the rest area.

An hour later, suddenly, and briefly, Marius became alert. Ella examined the tube and noted that his kidneys had stopped working. He was agitated, and she realised he was pointing at his collection of the figures involved in 'The Alamo'. He quickly relapsed into a deep sleep and Ella was left alone with her anger. She should have made a better effort to locate Santa Anna. It was his last wish and she had failed him. She tried to stop her emotional guilt but she was crushed with remorse. As Marius continued to sleep, she went over to the window, looked down the avenue of trees leading to the lake, and thought about Harry.

What were the five Anna Karenina principles that he had taught her? All had to be present for a relationship to work. The last was their undoing. She had allowed herself to chase her dreams with a man she had met outside a toy shop in Regent Street. She had neglected her responsibilities to her family and she had failed in the one request that Marius had made. She had dealt with things badly and now she was allowing events to tear Holly and Fred apart. She should have had time for him in the car park. He was soaking wet as a result of waiting for her. She shook her head in frustration.

It had been the right decision to bring Marius to London. There never was any real hope but they had to try.

She went back to the bedside and held her brother's hand. The blood seemed to be disappearing from his body. She looked up and watched Davy Crocket attempting to repel the Mexican army as the Alamo mission disintegrated around him. She placed Marius's hand by his side and walked back to the window. It was still raining but there were some streaks of early evening moonlight on the horizon.

She suddenly remembered the package that Harry had thrust into her hand. She went over to her coat and took out the small parcel from her pocket. She unwrapped it, and found herself holding a small figurine. It was President General Antonio Lopez de Santa Anna.

In that moment she knew that Harry was her Huckleberry friend, her 'Moon River' carefree partner.

She went over to the side of the bed and placed Santa Anna at the head of the Mexican army just as Marius opened his eyes. She held up the figure and watched him smile. His mouth opened and he and Ella laughed together.

Thirty minutes later, surrounded by his family, Marius van Houten passed away. In a last gesture he held out a skeletal arm and seemed to be trying to point towards General Santa Anna leading his Mexican soldiers who were reducing the Alamo mission to a burning funeral pyre as all the Texan defenders died.

Ella finally managed to persuade her family to get into the taxi and go back to their hotel rooms. The torrential rain continued, but she was oblivious to external events. She did not even put on a raincoat. She gave a final wave and decided to walk down to the lake in the grounds of the clinic. The combination of her tears, the rain, and the darkness reduced her visibility but were offset by the lights on either side of the pathway.

She was clinging to that final smile given to her by Marius as he realised that Santa Anna had joined the battle. She was now alone. She had counselled many patients on how to deal with bereavement; it was not quite the same when dealing with your own loss.

She so regretted the way she had treated Harry but she had no choice. It was right to ensure that Marius had departed as comfortably as possible. She silently applauded the pain management skills of the staff at the clinic.

There would be a rebuilding period with Harry. She managed to smile as she remembered his mannerisms. She wanted to know how he had located Santa Anna. That lay in the future. She thought about George and loved his way of contacting her on the 'DigiGo.' She was beginning to shiver and realised that she needed to go home. She looked across the lake; an island in the middle was illuminated. She became aware that, ahead of her, was a figure.

As the gap narrowed, she suddenly found that she was in his arms. Harry had waited for her. He had given her space to deal with her family. He had completed the fifth of the Anna Karenina principles and they were finally together. She clung to him with all her strength and their lips met. There was a flash of lightning and a thunder clap shook the area. The rain washed away the final memories of Holly and Fred. The only remaining link was a silver pendant hanging around her neck. Ella's future was now to have more lunches with Harry.

"Ik denk echter dat je geluk meisze," she said to herself.

She was, indeed, a lucky girl.

"Two drifters off to see the world
There's such a lot of world to see
We're after the same rainbow's end, waiting, round the bend
My Huckleberry friend, Moon River, and me".

THE END

Note 1: 'The story of 'Breakfast at Tiffany's"

The film is based on Truman Capote's novella (1958). Capote himself was a 5ft 3in controversial socialite who inflicted self-destruction when he wrote his intended fictional masterpiece 'Answered Prayers'. It was an exposure of the rich and powerful and their secrets. New York's fashionable doors became closed to him. He aged quickly due to drink and drugs abuse. He was openly homosexual. He was a close friend of Harper Lee. He died in 1984 aged fifty-nine. He wrote 'Breakfast at Tiffany's' when he was thirty-four.

The 1961 film, directed by Blake Edwards, grossed $14m. It propelled Audrey Hepburn to greater stardom although she was only ever nominated for a best actress award. The film won two Oscars: 'Best Original Score' and 'Best Original Song'. This, in itself, was ironic in that Paramount Pictures wanted to drop the Johnny Mercer/ Henry Mancini song until Hepburn said, "Over my dead body".

George Peppard plays Paul Varjak. He is a struggling writer who pays his way by bedding an older woman. He moves into an apartment block and quickly becomes involved with the quirky, temperamental, stunningly beautiful Holly Golightly. She calls him 'Fred', who is actually her brother. He is in the army and dies later in the film. Other story lines can be convoluted. There is a suggestion Holly is a hooker. She is paid to visit a hoodlum in prison who gives her unlikely weather forecasts. She is later arrested on suspicion of passing secret information.

In fact, the sub-plots are mostly implausible as are the characters, reflecting Truman Capote himself. The portrayal by Mickey Rooney of the landlord, Mr. I Y. Yunioshi, is ludicrous and Blake Edwards himself said it was a great mistake. Holly's cat is fun.

What holds the film together is the tantalising performance of Audrey Hepburn and the theme music, with her solo of 'Moon River' simply wonderful. And, at its heart, is a simple love story. The scene in Tiffany's, when George Peppard tries to buy Holly a present for under $10, is brilliant. The film ends with the famous kiss in pouring rain with the cat having been rescued from a trashcan in a sidewalk.

In 2004, 'Moon River' was voted the fourth most memorable song in Hollywood history by the American Film Institute. In 2012, the film was deemed 'culturally, historically or aesthetically significant' by the US Library of Congress. During 2016, it was staged across UK theatres with Pixie Lott playing Holly Golightly.

+

The sub-title, 'When I find out what I want, I'll let you know', comes from the film. The words are spoken by Hollywood agent, O. J. Berman, who is trying to explain Holly's character to Paul and repeats her own words to him.

Note 2: 'Santa Anna: the story of the Alamo'

Antonio Lopez de Santa Anna Perez de Lebron (1794 -1876), otherwise known as Santa Anna, was promoted to the rank of general in 1821 and was president of Mexico eleven times between 1833 and 1855. A man of charm, energy and political ability, he dominated the turbulent times for some thirty-five years. He was also vain and unprincipled and led his country to disaster. While successful against the Spanish in 1829 he was, on 20 April 1836, defeated by General Sam Houston heading the Texan army, at the Battle of San Jacinto. This led to Texas declaring itself to be independent. In December 1845 it was annexed by the United States of America.

At the end of the battle of San Jacinto there was carnage as the Texans, shouting, "Remember the Alamo", swept through the Mexican camp committing ghastly atrocities. As the soldiers surrendered, they threw their arms into the air shouting, "Me no Alamo". They were killed on the spot. 650 died and 700 escaped only to be captured and executed a few days later; only a few survived.

Santa Anna was found shivering in a swamp trying to pose as a common soldier. He was hauled in front of General Sam Houston where he complimented his rival and suggested that, "Now it remains for you to be generous to the vanquished". Sam Houston snarled his reply: "You should have remembered that at the Alamo". Yet, despite urgings from his staff officers, Houston did not execute his foe. Santa Anna agreed he would order his other commanders to retreat and cross back over the Rio Grande. He was allowed to return home to a political future.

Less than seven weeks earlier, the Alamo church fell as the defenders followed their orders to stand firm against overwhelming odds. As Santa Anna strolled amongst the smouldering corpses, he said "…these are the chickens, much blood has been shed, but the battle is over: it was but a small affair". It is thought that 257 men died defending the fort. Mexican casualties were around 600.

The siege of the Alamo, located at San Antonio, lasted from 23 February to 6 March 1836. Situated by the Medina River, the three acre mission stood in the way of the Mexican army's push through Texas. It was commanded by 26-year-old William Travis who believed he could hold out until reinforcements arrived. Unfortunately, the Texan Government had ceased to exist and Sam Houston was temporarily without authority. When Santa Anna attacked the mission, a convention was taking place at Washington-on-the-Brazos. The new Government declared independence from Mexico. General Houston did not take command of the Alamo relief force until five days after it had fallen.

Some did reach the Alamo before the attack took place. Jim Bowie, said to be 'a true son of the frontier', was a famed knife fighter who died trying to resist from his sickbed. Davy Crocket was a 49-year-old Indian fighter, and three-term US congressman, who arrived with his men to defend the palisade between the church and the south wall. Despite

Hollywood's best efforts it is not known where he died although it is certain it was in the mission.

Today, the Alamo is the main tourist attraction in Texas comprising manicured lawns, fishponds, and towering trees. The site is maintained by the Daughters of the Republic of Texas. See www.thealamo.org

+

Look out for more in the 'Novella Nostalgia' series

If you would like to be notified when the next book is released, be sure to sign up for my free newsletter at:

tonydruryemailsign-up.gr8.com

ALSO BY TONY DRURY

Sarah Rudd City Thriller series

Megan's Game: getBook.at/Megan

The Deal: getBook.at/Deal

Cholesterol: getBook.at/TDCholesterol

A Flash of Lightning: getBook.at/Lightning

The Lady Who Turned: getBook.at/TheLady

Sarah Rudd stories

On Scene and Dealing: the early career of DCI Sarah Rudd

Journey to the Crown: the Career of DCI Sarah Rudd from 2003 – 2008

Sarah Rudd Short Stories

The Contract Killer: getBook.at/CKiller

The Killer Who Missed: getBook.at/killerwhomissed

Stories written for HEART UK – The Cholesterol Charity. (All publisher's profits are paid to the charity)

Hannah's Choice

Joanna's Choice: getBook.at/JoannasChoice

Mark's Choice: getBook.at/MarksChoice

The Dinner Party

The Novella Nostalgia Series

Lunch with Harry

THE NOVELLA NOSTALGIA SERIES

This publishing initiative brings together the uniqueness of the novella and various memorable movies from the history of cinema.

The word 'novella' comes from the Italian for 'novel.' It has been interpreted in various ways including 'a long short story' or a 'short novel'. It can be traced back to the early renaissance in Italy and France. Giovanni Boccaccio wrote 'The Decameron' in 1353. This comprises 100 tales of ten people fleeing the black death. It was not until the 18th and 19th centuries that the novella emerged as a literary genre.

In 1941, the Austrian novelist Stefan Zweig wrote 'The Chess Novella' which was later renamed 'The Royal Game'. This was the inspiration for the 1960 film 'Brainwashed'.

Most modern novellas are published by Penguin Modern Classics. The various novella prizes seem to stipulate a word count of between 7,500 and 40,000. A key feature of the novella is its limited punctuation. There are no chapter headings and no breaks apart from spaces where the author needs to show a scene change.

+

'Lunch with Harry' pays tribute to one of the great films produced by Hollywood. Made in 1961, *'Breakfast at Tiffany's'* was based on the novella written by Truman Capote. It produced a mesmeric performance by Audrey Hepburn.

The modern tale is transferred to London and

features the charismatic Ella van Houten and Harry, who is guilt ridden following the death of his wife. They meet in Regent Street in unusual circumstances. Their growing relationship parallels their search for a model of the Mexican general, Santa Anna, who burned 'The Alamo' to the ground.

The second publication, scheduled for April 2017, is **'Twelve Troubled Jurors'** with echoes of '*12 Angry Men*' which gave the film world one of Henry Fonda's greatest performances.

This will be followed by **'Forever on Thursdays'** which hints at the unforgettable British film '*Brief Encounter*'. The love affair between Celia Johnson and Trevor Howard remains an icon in film history.

+

Full details of the Novella Nostalgia series can be found at www.cityfiction.co.uk

ABOUT TONY DRURY

Tony is the author of five DCI Sarah Rudd City thrillers. In each, he draws upon his career as a London financier to expose the underworld of dark practices and shadowy characters. None, however, are able to withstand the bravery and incisive detection methods of one of the police force's bravest officers. Her juggling of career demands, husband, children and her own demons, make riveting reading.

He has now written two more novels which trace the early career of probationary police constable Sarah

Whitson. In 'On Scene and Dealing' she meets her future husband Nick. In 'Journey to the Crown' she has a devastating affair with Dr Martin Redding. The final chapter jumps ahead to sample her future life as a private detective.

Tony has created an innovative series as a novella writer. Reflecting iconic cinema classics, his first is 'Lunch with Harry', which is inspired by 'Breakfast at Tiffany's'. Others to follow include 'Twelve Troubled Jurors' (echoing '12 Angry Men') and 'Forever on Thursdays' (capturing the drama of 'Brief Encounter').

He writes short-stories wherein the net proceeds go to HEART UK – The Cholesterol Charity. He is an ambassador for the charity.

Aged seventy, Tony is a follower of the wisdom of Albert Einstein: "When a man stops learning, he starts dying." He lives in Bedford with his wife Judy. They value every trip down the M1 to Watford to be with Grandson Henry.

Connect with Tony online:

(e) tony@cityfiction.co.uk
(w) tonydrury.com
Twitter: mrtonydrury
Facebook: facebook.com/tony.drury.author
Goodreads: goodreads.com/TonyDrury